RUBY'S HOPE

A Story of How the Famous "Migrant Mother" Photograph Became the Face of the Great Depression

Monica Kulling

illustrated by Sarah Dvojack

PAGE
STREET
KiDS

Ruby and her family were slow to leave Oklahoma.

In 1929, the stock market crashed. Millions lost their savings, their jobs, and their homes. Then came the drought. The ground grew nothing but thistles and dust. Dust buried tractors, killed cattle, and billowed into blizzards that turned day into night.

Years later, food was getting harder to find. Leaving seemed to be the only thing left to do.

Ruby was seven. Her older brother Leroy and sister Viola were keen to go. But Ruby didn't want to budge. She loved big-sky Oklahoma. The babies, Katherine and Norma, were quiet on the subject.

Ruby was watering a thistle that grew near the house.
She had once had baby chicks to feed, but they'd all died.

"Don't waste water on that weed, Ruby," said Ma, fighting with the wind to hang a line of wash. "Weeds are tougher than we are."

"Got that right," said Pa, resting on the front steps. "Time we were gone."

"Annie Folker's staying," said Ruby. "Her pa says one day the skies will split wide and rain's gonna fall and never stop."

"That may happen," said Ma. "But we won't be here to see it."

One morning, Ruby woke to find everyone busy. Pa and Leroy were fixing the car. Ma and Viola were packing up the kitchen.

"Ruby, mind the babies," said Ma. "We're leaving today."

"So soon?" asked Ruby. She felt her stomach drop. It was all happening too fast!

The Hudson Super-Six was packed tightly with everything needed to live on the road: a lantern, pots to cook and wash in, a big fry pan and coffee pot, plates and cups, spoons, knives and forks, clothes, and tools. Two mattresses held it all down.

It was time to hit the road. Ma and the babies sat in front. Leroy and Viola sat up top. Only Ruby wasn't budging.

She was standing still, staring at the farm.
"Stop your dreaming, Ruby," said Ma.
"They've got blue skies in California too."

"Come on," urged Viola.

Ruby wanted to remember every detail of
the place she had always called home.

When she was ready, Leroy and Viola hauled Ruby up, and the car rumbled west toward Route 66—the road that crossed the country.

It took two weeks and many flat tires to reach
the rich fields of California.

Ruby couldn't get over how green everything was!

Straight off, the family had found work picking lettuce. When they heard about a pea crop ready for picking outside of a town called Nipomo, they pointed the car in that direction.

"We may run out of gas," said Pa.

"We'll get to the camp even if we have to drive on fumes or push the truck," said Ma, with a determined look.

It sometimes seemed to Ruby that Ma pushed hope to its limits.

Lying on the mattress, Ruby gazed at the drifting clouds. Out of the blue, she said, "Lettuce makes me sick." They'd picked lettuce for over a week.

"You'll soon be saying the same thing 'bout peas," said Viola.

"Picking anything is tough work," agreed a yawning Leroy.

It was especially hard for Ruby, who wasn't strong. But she tried her best. She was helping, and that made her happy.

Pa drove the sputtering Hudson onto the dirt road, and that's where the gas ran out. The car coasted to a stop just inside the camp.

The next morning, Ruby woke to the feel of icy air in her nose and mouth. There had been a hard frost overnight and the pea crop was ruined.

"What'll we do now, Pa?" asked Leroy.

"We'll try and get work in town," replied Pa. "Then we'll move on."

In nearby Nipomo, Pa and Leroy took any job going—even street sweeping!

Days passed and food dwindled.
Ruby's hope dwindled too.

But not Ma's! Every day she cooked a bit extra so that the kids who crowded round their campfire might get a bite or two.

Ruby was the first to see the car and the woman with the black box.

"My name's Dorothea," she said, shaking Ruby's small hand.
"This is my camera. What's your name?"

"Ruby."

"How long have you been in this camp, Ruby?" asked Dorothea.

Ruby didn't often talk to strangers, but this lady seemed kind and eager to listen. Ruby told the photographer about leaving the farm where the trees, the garden, and the animals had all died. "Now the peas are dead too, our food is running out, and we have no money for gas."

"Don't lose hope, Ruby," said Dorothea. "When I was your age, I got a disease that left me with a twisted foot. I thought I'd never walk again. But here I am!"

Ruby had noticed the limp.

"Why are you carrying a camera?"

"The government hired me to take photographs of migrant farm workers."

Suddenly, Ruby had an idea. "Would you like to take my mama's picture?"

Dorothea wanted to, so Ruby led her toward the family's lean-to.
They skirted a large icy pond. The photographer walked slowly,
but Ruby ran ahead.

"Ma, this lady wants to take our picture!"

Dorothea Lange introduced herself. She told Ma about the government program that gave photographers like herself work recording the damage done to farmers by the Depression.

"May I take your picture? People who see it will realize how hard life is for migrant workers."

Ma gave the stranger a long, hard look. Her clothes weren't new, but neither were they dirty and torn. And her voice sounded big city.

But the photographer's eyes were kind so Ma agreed. "Take your pictures, though I don't see what good they'll do. We need gas to leave this place. We need food, not photographs."

Dorothea worked slowly and carefully. She put Ma at ease by talking about her own children—whom she hadn't seen in a month—all the while inching closer.

Dorothea Lange took six pictures, one after the other, then got back into her car and left.

The most famous of the six came to be called "Migrant Mother."

When the photograph of the mother with three of her children made the newspapers, people opened their hearts. Again, Ruby was the first to spot the trucks the day they rolled into camp. They brought 20,000 pounds of food and something more precious—hope.

AUTHOR'S NOTE

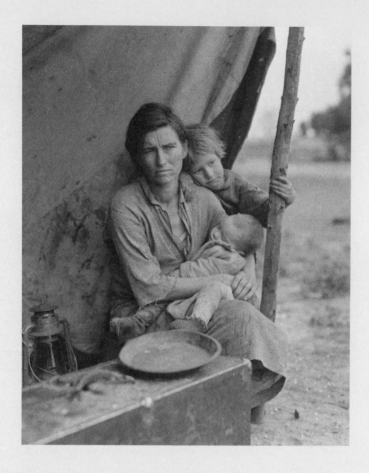

Ruby's Hope is based on real people and an actual event: the day Dorothea Lange took a photograph of a migrant farm worker and three of her children. This book is historical fiction. In my story I've used the names of the family members, but reimagined the events leading up to the taking of the photograph. For example, Ruby didn't lead Dorothea Lange to her mother, Florence Owens Thompson; but rather, Lange found her subject. "I saw and approached the hungry and desperate mother, as if drawn by a magnet." When the photo was taken, Thompson's husband (who in this story is a composite of multiple real-life characters) and two of her sons had gone to town to get a part to fix the car's radiator.

BIBLIOGRAPHY

Brown, Don. *The Great American Dust Bowl*. Boston: Houghton Mifflin Harcourt, 2013.

Burns, Ken, dir. *The Dust Bowl*. 2012; Arlington, VA: Public Broadcasting Service, 2012. DVD.

Egan, Timothy. *The Worst Hard Time: The Untold Story of Those Who Survived the Great American Dust Bowl.* Boston: Houghton Mifflin Harcourt, 2006.

Freedman, Russell. *Children of the Great Depression*. New York: Clarion, 2005.

Sprague, Robert and Oleta Kay Sprague Ham. *Migrant Mother: The Untold Story: A Family Memoir.* Mustang: Tate Publishing, 2013.

Stanley, Jerry. *Children of the Dust Bowl: The True Story of the School at Weedpatch Camp*. New York: Crown Publishers, 1992.

Taylor, Dyanna, dir. *Dorothea Lange: Grab a Hunk of Lightning*. 2014; Arlington, VA: Public Broadcasting Service, 2014. DVD.

How the "Migrant Mother" Came to Be

In 1933, when Franklin Delano Roosevelt became the thirty-second president of the United States, he created a number of programs to help America recover from the Great Depression. One was called the Farm Security Administration (FSA). It helped poor farmers, sharecroppers, and migrant workers.

During those bleak years of the dust bowl and failed crops, approximately 200,000 people migrated to California to make a better life for themselves and their children.

In 1935, the FSA hired photographers to travel to rural areas to record what life was like for these farmers and their families. Dorothea was one of those photographers.

Dorothea Lange was born in Hoboken, New Jersey, in 1895. When she was seven, she got polio. She recovered but walked with a limp for the rest of her life.

At age seventeen, Dorothea announced to her mother and brother that she wanted to become a photographer. She had never taken a picture in her life and didn't even own a camera!

Years later, Dorothea lived in San Francisco and had her own photography studio. One day, during the Great Depression, she decided to stop taking portraits and to turn her attention toward those who were suffering.

Early in 1936, Dorothea was driving home from an assignment when she passed a sign for a pea picker's camp near Nipomo in California. She kept driving, but twenty minutes later, on a whim, she suddenly turned her car around.

In the camp, Dorothea was drawn to a mother sitting with her children in a makeshift tent. Of the six photographs she took, the last one—"Migrant Mother"—is still the most recognizable image of the Great Depression. When it appeared in the newspapers, it made the country aware that there were 2,500 to 3,500 starving workers in a camp in California. Within days, the camp received 20,000 pounds of food from the federal government. In real life, however, the family had already moved on when the food arrived.

The woman sitting in the tent with her children was a Native American of the Cherokee Nation. She was born in Oklahoma in 1903. When Florence Owens Thompson died in 1983, the words on her gravestone were "Migrant Mother: A Legend of the Strength of American Motherhood."

For Nancy, first reader par excellence.

Thank you to Kristen Nobles for her invaluable comments on my first draft;
to Courtney Burke for being a pleasure to work with; and a special thank you to my agent
Karen Grencik for her kind perseverance. This project received a Writers' Reserve grant
from the Ontario Arts Council, for which I am grateful.
—M.K.

For my grandma, Melva.
—S.D.

Text copyright © 2019 Monica Kulling
Illustrations copyright © 2019 Sarah Dvojack

First published in 2019 by Page Street Kids,
an imprint of Page Street Publishing Co.
27 Congress Street, Suite 105
Salem, MA 01970
www.pagestreetpublishing.com

Distributed by Macmillan sales in Canada by The Canadian Manda Group

19 20 21 22 23 CCO 5 4 3 2 1

ISBN-13: 978-1-62414-818-7 ISBN-10: 1-6-2414-818-2
CIP data for this book is available from the Library of Congress.

This book was typeset in IM Fell English Pro.
The illustrations were drawn with graphite and colored digitally.
Printed and bound in Shenzhen, Guangdong, China.

Page Street Publishing uses only materials from suppliers who are committed to
responsible and sustainable forest management.

Page Street Publishing protects our planet by donating to nonprofits like The Trustees,
which focuses on local land conservation.